The Alphonso Rap

a novella

Jeffrey Hillard

Cover design by Jennifer Holbrock

ISBN – 978-0-9970365-2-7

Printed in the United States of America Library of Congress Cataloguing-in-Publication Data

Hillard, Jeffrey

The Alphonso Rap (A Shine in Bedlam Novella) – 1st Edition

For my sister, Jacqui Slabach

& For William Schutzius

SWEETS

IT WAS 1967 AND THE smell of cherry incense drifted throughout the store. It floated toward the snack rack. The smell weaved its way toward the cold bin and colas. It landed near the lettuce and carrots. All of these items were arranged near one another on narrow aisles that provided even narrower walking room.

Alphonso Peace worked as a clerk and stock-boy in this small grocery store. Nineteen-sixty-seven: incense was popular. Alphonso knew that young white child buying lettuce, apples, and bread for his mother brought in the scent. Nineteen-sixty-seven, and the war poured the strangest news into every town. Young boys, newly drafted to fight in Vietnam, kissed and hugged their mothers, fathers, and girlfriends on concrete porches before they left for the airport.

The war poured strange habits into Bedlam, too. Known for its massive perimeter of factories operating at full capacity twenty-four hours a day, Bedlam was also fragmented. White neighbors living in the north side of Bedlam and in a place known as Mudtown were distant from stores on the west side of Bedlam like Bettman's Grocery. Yet, white neighbors would shop at Bettman's and black residents in west Bedlam frequented Hattendorf's Grocery in north Bedlam, or Lawrence's in Mudtown.

A strangely divided town, and a strangeness that seemed to work.

It could confuse anyone, these neighborhoods.

But that boy wasn't confused in Bettman's, buying his mother's lettuce. Nor was Alphonso confused: that boy smelled like incense.

Alphonso walked over to him with his push-broom and took a whiff. The boy flinched at Alphonso's stare and walked up to old man Bettman at the cash register. He paid for his mother's lettuce, apples, and bread, left the store without buying any candy in the huge barrels by the register, and hopped on his bike.

Alphonso fetched a can of Lysol from old man Bettman's tiny office closet. He sprayed down the two aisles in the store where the incense lingered. He aimed the can high above the produce, the snack rack and the bread. Once he finished, he went up to the register.

"That boy smells funny every time he comes in here with his mama's list," Bettman said. "He smelled like pipe tobacco last week."

"Week before that like rotten eggs," Alphonso said.

"At least the kid says his mother says I have the best apples around."

Alphonso prepared to leave for the day. His four-hour shift was over. It was nearing six o'clock and dinner time. Mr. Bettman urged him to take a pound of sliced turkey home to his mother.

"She's not been feeling all up to par, lately, and she don't eat much meat anyhow," Alphonso said. "Mainly vegetables and rolls."

"That's a shame she's missing out on good meat," Bettman said. "It could give her more energy if she's parading those protest signs everywhere, those black power, civil rights signs she makes."

"She talked about moving up toward Washington D.C., where she can work in these black protests. She talking about equal rights, civil rights every time she talks. Her and her new Black Panther Party boyfriend. He got that strut."

"She needs energy. Good turkey or beef will give it if she's planning to do those protests all over creation."

"That why she talks about D.C.," Alphonso said, "where the real action is."

Before he could leave, the father of Alphonso's on-again, off-again girlfriend walked in, twisting his ball cap, forcing it to sit on his bald head. Head like a bowling ball, Alphonso thought. Rufus T. Jones cast a gruff presence. He was always an imposing presence to Alphonso. His girlfriend, Fortunate Jones, seemed to be her father's favorite. Although since Rufus had been living away from home in his own apartment these past eight months, Fortunate saw much less of him.

Rufus T. Jones casually blocked the front door.

"Hey, 'Phonso, you up to, man?"

Mr. Bettman said a quick hello and sped toward the cereal to count the remaining boxes for his daily inventory. He wanted no part of Rufus Jones' approach to Alphonso. Rufus hovered over Alphonso. It became a harmless staring contest. Alphonso blinked, looked out the front window.

"Ain't nothing happening, Mr. Jones."

"Where I ask about anything happening with my daughter?"

"You're looking at me kind of funny."

"But I'm not funny, right?" Rufus said.

Alphonso did not have to read Rufus Jones' mind. He knew the man wanted him to realize he kept an account of when Alphonso saw his daughter and where he might take her, even if Rufus was separated from his daughter's mother.

Rufus took a hearing aid out of his right ear and shook it. He slipped it back into place and a wiry plastic brace around his ear.

"I hope this hearing aid ain't going bad. Did I hear you say you were going to cool it seeing Fortunate?"

"Not what I said. I said I take care of Fortunate."

"You mean take care of calling it quits one day soon," Rufus said, "so you don't ruin a good thing. That good thing is my daughter."

Rufus Jones winked, but it seemed to Alphonso like an ominous wink of one forbidding another to cross a certain line of action. Alphonso understood that wink coming from an adult. He witnessed that same wink from his political-activist mother. And it was not a friendly wink.

Rufus looked over at old man Bettman acting as if he was seriously counting the few boxes of Frosted Flakes and Cheerios on the shelf. "Hey, Bettman," he said, "where those peanuts you hiding?"

Without saying a word, Mr. Bettman pointed toward the front. After Rufus paid and left, whistling some song, Mr. Bettman pulled Alphonso toward the corner of the cold bin where milk products were stocked. He chastised Alphonso for pushing Rufus Jones to his limit. This was a mild-mannered grocery store owner who thrived on congeniality. An owner who knew nothing about the romantic admiration Alphonso had for Fortunate Jones.

"I'll number your days here you go messing up my store with some dude like that man Jones making trouble."

Alphonso said it was not trouble, nor was trouble brewing, and that Bettman should calm down. After listening to Bettman abruptly switch to some kid stealing his sweets near the door - his stash of candies in those huge barrels - Alphonso suddenly felt a surge of boldness himself. Probably no kid was stealing. Bettman was imagining it all.

That boldness took hold: he had worked hard for the benefit of a pack of peanuts that he had his eyes on. He would get paid Friday, but today was Monday and he was hungry. He walked over to the shelf with peanuts, snatched a bag, put it in his back pocket, and headed out the door. Not hurrying, either.

Alphonso opened those peanuts outside the door and in full view of Mr. Bettman who watched him walk up the street.

OWL

ALPHONSO COULD DRIVE, AND HE did
drive a lot, although of recent he couldn't find his Ohio
driver's license. It didn't faze him. He gripped the
steering wheel higher, with both hands, so that any cop
driving by would see that he was a conscientious
driver. He looked straight ahead. He didn't sweat
knowing his wallet contained no license.

He would drive Fortunate Jones to her friend Sheila
Dalryple's house nearly each week. She and Fortunate
were in the 12th grade; they had gone to Bedlam
together since second grade, so Fortunate's white
friend, Sheila, had no problem inviting her over to
listen to new albums, with bands like Diana Ross and
The Supremes, The Chi-Lites, The Lovin' Spoonful,
and Jefferson Airplane pumping out tunes that reached
the Top-Ten.

At this point in his life, for his girl Fortunate,
Alphonso would risk being pulled over by a Bedlam

7

cop in north Bedlam, who would then question Alphonso about his lost driver's license. Alphonso was unsure what lay ahead of high school. He had little interest in pursuing college. In fact, he was close to dropping out of high school. The teachers burdened students, you had to be a jock to get truly noticed, and you never knew when a teacher would single you out to humiliate you, even if you were totally finished with a homework assignment. Listening to Fortunate talk about the good pay at the Empire warehouse interested him.

His fixation was on a car. If he could keep driving, then that meant freedom. He liked knowing that Fortunate worked. She inspired him. She always carried single dollar bills in her purse.

Fortunate explained to him that she would not be long at Sheila's. They had cheerleading business to discuss, and they would listen to one side of the 1966 album, "The Supremes A 'Go-Go," with Diana Ross and The Supremes.

Alphonso yawned while gazing at a stout man talking to a tree. The man seemed agitated. He called to a tree limb. But, Alphonso soon spotted the cat in the tree. The cat lay balanced on a thick branch. It eyed the sky, the ground, and the roly-poly man with barely any neck.

Fortunate paid no attention to the man or his cat or Alphonso as he stepped out of his mother's 1963 Ford

Falcon. Fortunate hurried up to Sheila's front porch and met her at the door. Fortunate's friend exuded an excitable, athletic personality that helped her earn a spot on Bedlam High's cheerleading squad and enabled her to land countless friends. Fortunate and a girl named Tamara Key were two of Sheila's closest friends. She made sure they knew they were welcomed on her street, in predominantly white north Bedlam. They spent a good part of the summer, when they weren't working or practicing cheerleading, lounging at Sheila's, listening to The Supremes and The Temptations.

The stout man's name was Dick Topper. His brother was Cecil Topper, mayor of Bedlam. Both were short and both could easily get lost in a crowd. Dick Topper saw Alphonso watching the cat. Alphonso shaded his eyes with his forearm.

He motioned Alphonso to come over. "I've got to get this cat down," Topper said, as Alphonso approached the front yard tree.

"Look like you got a problem," Alphonso said. "Like your cat ain't moving."

"This one climbs up there about twice a year. When it escapes. In the cold of winter it's not funny."

"It's a indoor cat?"

"Not today. Not usually."

"You want me climb up? I can see if it comes to me."

9

Dick Topper paused before granting Alphonso permission. Alphonso removed his watch and set it on the edge of the sidewalk. When he started climbing he remarked to Dick Topper that he didn't care for cats, but since he was here, there was no harm in trying to rescue an animal. He had nothing to do but wait for his girlfriend. Good neighborly cause, he thought as he crawled on a tree limb. Even in this neighborhood which was foreign to Alphonso. He gently clutched the fur on the cat's neck. Alphonso was also thinking it would be very peculiar for another neighbor of Sheila's to look out a window and see a black boy climbing a tree in north Bedlam.

"Got it," he said.

"Come here, Owl," Topper said. "We named him Owl because he likes to roam the house at night."

Alphonso crawled backward gracefully on the limb, holding the cat under his arm. By that time, Dick Topper had scampered into his garage. He wobbled out with a step ladder. Standing on the top rung, he reached out with both hands and took the cat Alphonso handed to him.

Topper chatted in a rambling way, hardly hearing Alphonso slip from the branch and fall about five feet to the ground. He heard Alphonso moan. The moaning grew louder. And that's what prompted Topper to really react. He rushed his cat inside his house.

"Be right back," he said. "I'll bring ice."

Alphonso held his ankle with as much pressure as he could apply.

By the time Topper returned with a bag of ice cubes, Alphonso was leaning on the hood of his car. He limped toward a strip of grass along the curb where he sat and wrapped the bag around his ankle.

He noticed Fortunate and Sheila seeming to argue on the side porch. He couldn't make out what they were saying. He tried. He tilted his head, hoping to make out what Fortunate was saying. He vaguely heard the words, "Emerald" and "jewelry," and that's all. The girls began to walk toward the Galaxy.

Sheila again raised her voice, and now Alphonso could better hear her: "If Emerald puts in too many more hours at the jewelry store, she'll lose out on cheerleading once and for all. She'll get cut. She's great, but coach won't see her as committed. You know coach. Cheerleading or nothing. I have to tell Mr. Topper, but I don't want to get Emerald in trouble."

"Then don't," Fortunate said. "Let Emerald handle herself. Let her deal with Dick Topper. She's overworked. But she can decide what she wants."

"I don't know that she wants to act," Sheila said.

"Look, if some people are loitering around the store, and if some people are maybe casing the place, then that's not Emerald's problem. That's an owner's problem. Right over there," as Fortunate pointed to

11

Topper's house. "It's a cop problem. Emerald shouldn't feel responsible for being a look-out for a place that might even get robbed."

Dick Topper happened to own Topper's Jewelry store, the store Sheila and Fortunate argued over. For such a passionate argument, Alphonso thought it odd that Fortunate didn't attempt to walk right over to Topper and ask him why he was concerned that someone might be casing his store. Fortunate was generally quiet but bold. She said little, though she spoke her mind. Neither she nor Sheila walked over to Topper's house to ask him why he didn't insist that his brother the mayor alert the cops to more regularly cruise by Topper's store deep into the night, and keep a better eye on it.

Neither girl made that effort right now to ask Topper to hold off pressuring their friend Emerald Key.

Fortunate just said to Sheila, "If Emerald keeps complaining, she might wind up quitting the store."

"She's not quitting. Too good of pay," Sheila said. "He's just paranoid. That neighbor of ours thinks a necklace or ring will disappear into thin air. All Emerald does is clean jewelry, change the display cases, gets her boss' tools to make rings. She doesn't know anybody who'd be interested in stealing jewelry. Topper must be paranoid. He pressures her. But he pays good."

Dick Topper's wife came out the front door with a tray of five cupcakes. She offered the whole plastic tray to Alphonso and urged him to take them all. "You can eat them later," she said. "The tray's disposable."

As soon as she went back inside, Alphonso ate with one hand and held his ankle with the other hand. Fortunate and Sheila finally came over toward the tray and each grabbed a cupcake.

"What's up with you?" Fortunate said.

"I fell out of the tree getting that cat."

"Oh. You got it then. You got to be more careful next time you climb trees." Fortunate and Sheila laughed. They'd paused their apparent arguing in the yard. Alphonso's ankle had swollen, though he still insisted on driving.

Sheila went back into her house satisfied that she and Fortunate could support their friend Emerald. Alphonso's injured right ankle sharpened with pain when his right foot worked the accelerator and brake.

He winced even more when his quick stops jolted Fortunate's eating process. He knew she was biting into a cupcake when he braked. It pained him to watch those cupcake crumbs dribble all over the front seat and floor of his mother's Galaxy. He didn't want to think too deeply about how he'd have to hobble around with a vacuum cleaner and suck up every last crumb.

SPLIT

ALPHONSO STOOD AT THE OPENING of Rufus T. Jones' garage and watched Rufus' daughter, Fortunate, count hubcaps. The hubcaps were piled evenly in three tall stacks on the garage floor.

Rufus had been separated from Fortunate's mother for five months, but the garage was still partly his, and his work in the growing hubcap industry, as he'd termed it to his daughter, was blossoming. Rufus timed his visits to the garage when his near-ex-wife was at work. He had Fortunate or his oldest daughter, C. Adelle, communicate to him each week the exact working hours their mother was assigned. Their mother rarely walked into the garage. She parked in the driveway. Seeing Rufus' tools scattered all around unnerved their mother. Best, she said, to keep that garage door closed.

Fortunate had finished her shift counting inventory at the Empire warehouse in west Bedlam. With the garage door open, Alphonso saw the sunlight flank part of the garage where several brand new hubcaps had been tossed. He watched his girlfriend wipe each inch of a hubcap with a towel and Windex. She cleaned between grooves and notches. A number of the hubcaps looked like they fit Cadillacs and Buicks. Large, roomy cars with gleaming hoods that caught every angle of sunlight or pushed any hard rain off their paint jobs.

"You spiffing those up for Rufus?"

"I'm done," Fortunate said. "I quit this. I'm not and never will be a part of his scheme. It's wrong. Taking hubcaps off cars is dead wrong. He says every hubcap is twenty bucks, and he wants to see his face in them. Like a mirror. Not for me."

"What's he do? Sell them out of state?"

"He don't want me talking about his business. You know that. I turn a deaf ear to what he does."

A Ford station wagon pulled into the driveway. Two brothers, Troy and Terence Simms, got out and walked past Alphonso without saying a word. Troy took the lead, it seemed, and paced back and forth in the garage, while Terence rubbed his back against a garage corner and smoked a cigarette, his large sunglasses firmly covering the top half of his face.

"Girl, you doing good," Troy said. "We need eight caps for two other Fords. A delivery downtown."

Alphonso recognized the young man sitting in the

backseat as a senior at Bedlam High School named Hugh Willie. He looked out of place sitting in the backseat, waiting for the two, very new and inexperienced Black Panther Party members to load the hubcaps into the back and head out. For a white teen who was gangly and awkward, with a comical thin neck, Hugh Willie had an ungainly, teased-out afro. He was the only white guy in Bedlam, Alphonso knew, with that amount of naturally curly hair able to be transformed into a spacious afro. In fact, Hugh Willie's hair was more dazzling than Troy Simms' afro, which supported a pick-comb on one side above his ear and a pencil above the other ear.

Hugh Willie got out of the car and, herky-jerky with his steps, walked around nervously in front of Alphonso. Willie lit a Marlboro. He tossed one to the quieter of the two Simms brothers, sullen Terence Simms, who'd just squished his other cigarette against the garage. Terence lowered his sunglasses and stared at Alphonso.

"Your girl does a fine job bringing shine to the product," Terence said. He pushed up his sunglasses.

"She cool," Alphonso said. "But she quit. She's out of the spit-shine business."

"Cool, man? More than cool, you mean," Troy Simms said. "She's necessary. She's on top of it."

"Spit shine those rims," Terence Simms said, unusually chatty.

"Looking good here," Troy said.

"I quit, Troy," Fortunate said, standing near a corner with her arms folded.

Alphonso watched his girlfriend stare at Troy Simms. He handed four clean hubcaps to Hugh Willie who opened the back gate of the station wagon and laycred them on what looked like a velvet cloth. Hugh placed more velvet on top of each cap. He did the same with four more caps.

Inside the stifling aroma of cigarette smoke, the three guys whisked out of Rufus' driveway, turned up the radio to its loudest volume, and sped off. Fortunate held a push-broom out in front of Alphonso; he got the message. They would surely close that door before anyone else walked by.

Later that afternoon, as Alphonso got in his car to go to work at Bettman's, Fortunate stopped him from pulling away.

"Ok," she said, "I'll tell you two things. Keep them between us. Do not tell your mama. Number one, Hugh Willie knows everyone. He a talker. He knows every car in Bedlam, Mt. Relling, even Jefferson Heights. And he knows when they park their cars on the street in any neighborhood, and what time of night some certain unnamed people can strip hubcaps off a car. Hugh Willie's like an owl. He won't miss anything. He's a look-out. He also has some other people rip off those caps. And number two, the Simms brothers are selling that property to raise money for the local Black Panthers. Hugh Willie gets five bucks a cap. I told my father, 'No more.' This was my last stacking. I'm not aiding him and getting my mom in trouble, too. I said, 'I'll tell mom if you don't move your merchandise.'"

"He threaten you? Simms brothers threaten you?"

"Threaten me? Who you kidding? I'm stronger than what they think. I'm not playing."

"What about Rufus?"

"He just patted my back and said, 'Don't worry, I got another place all set up. You off the hook, sweet thing.' He better be right."

***

THE OLD MAN HUDDLED NEXT to a basket of apples and raised up as if he was expecting Alphonso. Bettman's Grocery was closed, but Alphonso entered through the unlocked back door.

Old man Bettman called him to the front of the store, as opposed to the crates of apples he was unloading. Alphonso took his time, dawdling, knowing he was sadly underpaid at three dollars an hour, and not relenting to the authority of the store owner. He stood for a moment admiring the various cereals. Bettman crossed his arms. Alphonso knew that when Bettman crossed his arms the old man was contemplating trouble.

"You want me?" Alphonso said.

"You can do something for me." Bettman worked a ball point pen around his head of gray hair, pecking at parts of his scalp.

"What's that?"

"You can not come back tomorrow."

"What's that, again?" Alphonso said.

"I'm letting you go."

"Why for?"

"Here, take this cash for two weeks' work, up to the end of next week." Bettman handed Alphonso a brown envelope.

"What happened, man? What I do?"

"I can't have you causing trouble, having that crazy man Rufus Jones coming in, threatening, having it out with you, dishing it out in my store. I don't know what you got going on with his daughter. If he's mad, he's mad. I don't want it trickling all into my store. I got paying customers. Plus, I don't trust where you're going with her. Around him, it could be trouble. This cash will hold you over."

When Alphonso opened the envelope to count sixty dollars in ten dollar bills, Bettman hurried to answer the ringing phone next to the cash register. He looked aimless. He motioned Alphonso over to the counter, handed him the phone, scowling at him. Alphonso, surprised Bettman even allowed him to use the phone, grabbed it with confidence. This was the last time he could let Mr. Bettman see him in control of an issue inside the man's store.

Alphonso made the call brief. Bettman still kept his arms crossed; only this time when he spoke, he offered unexpected sympathy.

"You ok? She ok?"

"All ok, man. That's Fortunate, my girl. I have to drive her again tomorrow. A kind of emergency. Has to do with those cheerleaders at Bedlam. Always something going on with those girls."

Alphonso now held the envelope tightly. He stuffed it into a pocket, as well as a fistful of Jolly Ranchers candy that Bettman gave him. Once outside, he heard the door lock behind him.

CASH

AS SOON AS ALPHONSO EASED his car in front of Sheila Dalryple's house in north Bedlam, a dog darted in front of it. Fortunate stuck her head out of the passenger's window and watched the dog sniff the car and scamper behind it and down the street.

The dog obviously sensed freedom because it didn't stop. However, Dick Topper stopped running toward it once he saw he had no chance corralling it. And once he saw Alphonso sitting in the car, he walked over like a man devising a serious plan. He shook his finger, as if relieved. Alphonso rolled down his window. Dick Topper wanted his attention.

"Want to help me get a dog now? You're awfully great with cats."

"I doubt I can get it, Mr. Topper. I'm not good with dogs."

"Sure we could. A team."

Alphonso was in no way going to insert himself in

21

the backyards of white residencies searching for a dog whose instinct was not to get caught. He leaned back in his car seat. Dick Topper seemed stunned. He bounced his fingers on the hood.

"I'll be right back," Topper said.

"Sheila and I will go search for your dog," Fortunate said.

Within fifteen minutes, Fortunate and her friend had taken two large steak bones that Sheila's father set aside for the Dalryple's own dog and bagged the bones. Once they saw the dog chase a cat in a yard at the end of the street, they took those bones out of the bag. Sheila waved one and Fortunate waved the other. The dog bolted toward the girls and somehow locked both bones between its sizable mutt's teeth, sat chewing like an obedient dog, and let Sheila fasten a leash to its collar. Captured. Secured for the walk back to Topper's.

In her bedroom, Sheila related to Fortunate her personal complaint about one of their co-cheerleaders-friends who had apparently attempted to steal Sheila's boyfriend a second time. Fortunate eventually got her friend to question whether her boyfriend was worth the anxiety, if he could so easily respond to this co-cheerleader's invitation. Anyway, the girl was tagged as a someone whom every cheerleader on Bedlam's squad suspected as a boyfriend thief.

Growing uncomfortable by the minute, Alphonso

hoped Fortunate would not take advantage of his long-suffering patience too much longer. He noticed Dick Topper carrying a piece of paper toward him. He turned down the radio volume. Stevie Wonder's song, "I Was Made to Love Her," was a whisper now. Dick Topper put his hand with the paper behind his back.

"Step out of the car, Alphonso. This will only take a minute. It's a yes or no question."

Alphonso got out and leaned against the car door. He blocked Dick Topper's full view of the front interior.

"I've got a kind of surprise, something to ask you about. For you to think about," Topper said.

"A surprise?"

"A big one. It comes with an offer, too."

"An offer?"

Topper explained how he believed in his own instincts, and they tended to be flawless. He said his instinct had pinpointed Alphonso as someone reliable. "You're on my radar," he said. Topper explained how a jewelry store operates, with finding the right ring fits, cleaning gems, and the overall maintenance required of personal expensive jewelry. Alphonso listened, biting a thumbnail. Topper was in need, he said, of a young worker who could help his best employee, Tamara Key, handle several tasks associated with jewelry store upkeep.

"I'd be interested. Real interested."

Alphonso almost revealed that he lost his job at Bettman's, but he caught himself in time to say, "I'm in between jobs, man. What can I do?"

Dick Topper gently pulled Alphonso's hand toward him, spread his fingers, and placed a twenty dollar bill on his palm. "Consider this up-front pay, a bonus pay already, because I also appreciated your getting down Owl out of the tree. I owe you."

"Appreciate that," Alphonso said, pocketing yet another twenty dollars. His silent calculation put his total for the last two days at eighty dollars. It was eighty dollars Fortunate had no idea about yet.

Dick Topper continued to rub his own fist. "Like this," he said. He held high his fist. "This hand is clean. I'm rubbing off any dirt. See, I like my store crystal clean, the gems sparkling, the customers happy, and a clean operation."

He put down his hands. "I got one worry. I sometimes see guys hanging out or angling around my store. Tamara can't watch the premises all day and do other work. I need more eyes."

"What guys?"

"I don't know. They wander around. They wander back and forth. They'll stare at the display cases in the window. How about twenty hours a week?

"Deal."

"I don't want to cause a stir. I thought maybe if you see certain guys you might spot as non-buyers, you might ask them to move on, keep the storefront clear."

"You want me to also look out and act as a kind of security guy while I'm also keeping up the store?"

"Sure. And a few other tasks. Good ones for you. Come by next Tuesday afternoon. Three o'clock. Tamara Key will show you the ropes."

"Deal."

TOPPER'S

TAMARA KEY, WHOSE NICKNAME WAS Emerald, led Alphonso into the vault where Dick Topper's surplus of fine jewelry was safely sealed. She had shown him how to arrange and re-arrange rings, necklaces, and bracelets in the storefront window displays. She ordered him to lift the velvet cases full of rings out of the in-store glass cases just the way she did. Mostly, he walked behind Emerald, hands clasped behind his back, winking at her every so often, enthralled with the reflection of glitz on the cases, fascinated that not one speck of dust or finger-smear tainted any of the glass.

Emerald's parents had begun calling her by her now-popular nickname when, at two-years old, a splotchy glow appeared on parts of her face, as if her cheeks emitted a kind of light. Her cheeks like two small lightbulbs. Tamara's parents had celebrated their third wedding anniversary that night and drank their fill of champagne. Tamara's mother first noticed her toddler-daughter's cheeks, because she was the more sober of the two. The babysitter straightened Tamara in front of her mother. Tamara's mother squatted. In disbelief, she saw how light-skinned - how brightly lit - Tamara's cheeks were in contrast to her dark skin. But to Tamara's mother, it was a pristine light, or lightness, or some weird apparition of glow only granted by the Good Lord and not by genes alone. She shut her eyes for over a minute, opened them, stared again at her daughter's cheeks, even her bright forehead. She ran her fingers across her daughter's forehead.

"It's not hot. No fever I can tell," she said.

"She played all night, never let up," the babysitter said.

Tamara's mother called to her husband. "Look at your girl, sweetheart. Look at her glow. She all glowing. I'm calling her Emerald. I'm Pearl. That's my name, my real name. My Tamara baby's going to be a fine gemstone name, a Emerald. She got a little green in her cheeks. I like that."

"You got it down, sugar," he husband said, wobbly drunk. "Sounds good to me. Got a ring to it. Smooth."

And there it was. Tamara Emerald Key. Mostly Emerald, except to her 70-year old grandmother who only called her Tamara, Little Miss Tamara.

At seventeen, Emerald Key was tall and lanky like

her mother. She used her long arms, when she pushed a broom, to cover at least six feet of floor space. She got done twice as fast, too.

Each time Emerald began to explain a new task to Alphonso, she placed a piece of jewelry in his hands and said, "Imagine being as careful with that precious item as you would holding an egg. You got that? Drop it and you gone. Topper will fire you he know you dropped anything, or you didn't do what he hired you to do. Which is mostly clean and straighten display cases."

Emerald could talk as one might expect a boisterous cheerleader could do. Cheerleaders like Emerald, Fortunate, and Sheila, to Alphonso, were born talkers. Although, interestingly, his own girl Fortunate often happened to be quiet to the point of muteness. She could almost be sullen. Fortunate eyed every moving object. She prided herself on studying a scene before she acted. Fortunate took herself seriously. At seventeen, and as a young female, she was the only Empire worker whom a supervisor with years of factory experience trusted to keep half of the Empire warehouse clean and orderly. Fortunate's supervisor even allowed her to determine her own break and lunch times. Alphonso's girlfriend was dependable and loyal.

At Topper's Jewelry, Emerald Key was frequently in charge. She pulled out a desk drawer which was loaded with small flowery Thank-You cards. Emerald had designed the cards' front side with ink sketches of a necklace and ring. In a corner of each card was the inscription: "Illustration by Emerald Key."

"You'll be filling these out and sending them to paying customers," she said.

"Nice work, girl."

"It takes time to draw. I don't have time anymore to write notes. I'll have a script for you. You just copy it into those cards. Maybe four to twenty a week. Depends on the week."

"I'll get a wrist cramp doing just one. And I don't like to write anything."

"But you will," she said, asserting her title of associate store clerk.

By the time Emerald showed him how jewelry was loaded into "palaces," or small rectangular boxes, at the end of a day, and before the palaces were placed in the vault, Alphonso noticed in the store a young man whose back was turned toward him. He watched Emerald cross the store and nearly step up to the young man's side. She stood with her hands on her hips, as if waiting to say something. The person did not move, did not make eye contact with her.

He looked down at the display case and said, pointing directly at one expensive diamond ring, "I'd like to see that one."

Emerald took her hands off her hips and confronted

him. "You'll see nothing," she said.

The guy with the wiry afro didn't react or look at Emerald. Only, he was a white male with an afro, and Alphonso recognized him as soon as he turned: Hugh Willie. He was wearing a padded jacket awkwardly large for his shoulders, though it was extremely humid outside.

"You got fired two weeks ago, Hugh," she said. "You're not suppose to be in here."

"I can't look around? Free country."

"Not when you got fired for not coming into work and not calling, and now look at you. You're in here loitering. It's not free."

Emerald poked Hugh Willie's jacket with her long fingers. Alphonso only now noticed she wore three different rings, each illuminating her slim fingers.

Alphonso walked over to the case. "What's going on, man?"

"You looking, too?" Willie said. "Nice stuff in here, if someone would let me look."

"Topper's in the back working on orders. You want him?" Emerald said.

Willie ignored her. "I thought you worked with Fortunate Jones," Willie said to Alphonso.

"That's my girlfriend's house you saw me at."

Although Alphonso was two inches taller than Hugh Willie, and looked down at him, Willie's afro made him seem tall. It was more perky that

30

Alphonso's hair, with its bouncy and frizzy curls, unevenly shaped.

"That's your girl, true? That's cool," Willie said. "But one thing."

"What's that?"

Hugh Willie nudged Alphonso toward an opposite corner of the store, away from Emerald. He touched Alphonso's elbow. Alphonso looked over his shoulder at Emerald moving behind the case. She reached inside it to re-arrange several boxes and a necklace hanging on propped-up styrofoam. She looked up and watched the two guys. Hugh Willie whispered into Alphonso's ear. Alphonso could sense Fortunate did her best to eavesdrop.

She even tried to interrupt the flow of conversation: "Hey, Willie, you want Mr. Topper to come out here and see you?"

And again he kept his focus on Alphonso, who became uncomfortable standing so close to a person who obviously was heavily involved in hubcap stealing.

"Best you not say anything about me at school when it starts, neither," he whispered to Alphonso. "What you seen in that car wasn't mine to begin with. Fortunate's dad owns a bunch. I was just along for the ride. I like to ride along with people. I like cars. Simms are my black brothers. They let me ride. I dig their friendship. Peace, man."

31

Alphonso wanted to raise questions: Why did you look so interested in the hubcaps going into that station wagon? And as you said, it was your father's car, so why was Troy Simms driving your father's car, and why did Terence Simms seem so confident and bright-eyed watching Fortunate stand next to those hubcaps? What do you know about where those caps are going? And do you get paid by the Simms brothers or by Rufus T. Jones, if you get paid at all?

Questions abounded. Alphonso deferred to his more cautious self: do not get any more involved than you are, which right now is guilt by association. You, Alphonso, are associated with Rufus T. Jones because you date his beautiful, quiet, hard-working daughter.

In the span of three minutes in which Hugh Willie captured Alphonso's attention, so many questions reared up in his mind. Alphonso slapped them down. Emerald Key's patience had plummeted. Here came Dick Topper approaching the two guys.

"Mr. Willie, do I need to call the Bedlam police?" Topper said.

"Hey, Topper, I was shopping," he said.

"Let me go to my phone."

With that, a swoosh. Willie's oversize jacket whisked against the wall and the front door chimed as he nearly ran outside. Two new customers walked in. Dick Topper himself escorted the man and woman to a case of engagement rings. All the prior banter and tension vanished in a flash.

***

AS IF BEING CONFRONTED BY Hugh Willie wasn't enough excitement for Alphonso.

He did not expect to confront his own mother lying on the floor of their living room, holding a washrag on her forehead, her other hand clutching her chest.

Alphonso's mother forbid her son to call for a Bedlam ambulance. "It's indigestion, that's all," she said, scraping her knees along the carpet in a move to get up. "Help me up to my couch, that's all I need."

Alphonso brought her a glass of water. He insisted on calling the police station to ask for an ambulance if her breathing didn't adjust more evenly to calmer exhalations. He gave her body ten minutes to adjust. She sat up on the couch, finally. She waved off her son. She asked for more water. "That water is like wine," she said.

But, Alphonso also noticed in the living room a strange absence below his mother's poster of Black Panther, Huey Newton. Her other protest posters were missing. There were at least ten she'd collected. She had spent weeks this summer of 1967 spray-painting slogans on cardboard like, "Power and Equality," "Power to the People," and "Mass Non-Violent Direct Action Will Save the World."

"Where your posters?"

"In the bedroom. I'm done," she said. "I'm giving them to my boyfriend to take forever."

"Why?"

"I ain't feeling well with these headaches. I don't feel like going to Detroit or Chicago right now. Folk up there can protest on their own," she lectured Alphonso. "They can form their own power, which they're doing by the day. Black Panthers helping organizing classrooms for real education outside the public schools. Radical folks marching, even whites, and bringing volunteer nurses into places to help with kids and old black folk who can't get to a hospital. Everyone on the move except these politicians."

Alphonso took in his mother's lecture on the positive nature of her protests. Politicians were taking notice, she said, even though they were lazy, all except for the Kennedy family. His mother, catching her breath, also said about those politicians that they were finally taking notice of her friends' fight to recognize the equal rights of women who could work in a workplace just as successfully as men.

She ran out of energy and fell asleep in front of him. He drew a blanket across her shoulders.

He let her sleep without repositioning her neck, which was uncomfortably drooping across a couch cushion.

He walked into her bedroom to admire once again

the artfulness she'd put into creating her protest posters' lettering, but he noticed they were already gone.

LOT

WHEN ALPHONSO WALKED EMERALD KEY to her car parked in the back of Topper's Jewelry, he stopped listening to her endlessly describe the sale of a one-thousand-dollar diamond Dick Topper made to an 75-year old man. It was a wedding ring for the man's 72-year old fiance.

While Emerald looked at the sky, talking feverishly, Alphonso once and for all tuned her out and gazed in the direction of that unkempt afro sported by Hugh Willie. Emerald drove off, still talking to herself, and not spotting Hugh Willie. Alphonso watched him cut grass in a vast yard across the alley behind Topper's.

Skinny Hugh Willie struggled pushing a lawn mower nearly as heavy as he was. Midway through cutting, Willie let the lawn mower die. He left it in the middle of the mostly vacant uncut yard. Alphonso ducked behind another car in the alley, out of Willie's sight. He inched his head above a side mirror and glimpsed Hugh Willie walking through the parking lot of an apartment complex. Hugh strolled back and forth. He could have been searching for a particular car. He paused in front of four or five cars. He wrote on the back of his hand with a pen. Alphonso suspected Hugh Willie was recording car makes and models and license plate numbers. Hugh squatted at one car, a 1965 Ford Fairlane, and felt around each tire. He strangely pulled off one hubcap and put it right back on. He shrugged his shoulders.

Alphonso watched him feel around the rim of a 1965 Ford Mustang coupe. He also watched a Bedlam Police car when the officer spied the lawn mower alone in the middle of the yard. He recognized the officer. Elmer Klump. Klump also went by the nickname "Breezy." Breezy Klump smoked long menthol cigarettes most of the day as he cruised Bedlam on his day shift.

Breezy Klump sat in his cruiser and waved Hugh Willie over. Hugh, without hesitating, hid his inked hand from view. Alphonso could see Breezy blow cigarette smoke in Willie's direction, causing the kid to step back further. His cigarette dangled from his lips as he talked. Willie kept scooting back inch by inch until, after a series of anxious hand motions, he strutted away from Breezy and restarted his lawn mower.

Someone came around the corner from Topper's Jewelry store and stood next to Alphonso. He stretched his legs after kneeling so long. The voice of Troy Simms so startled him that he straightened up quickly. As if he owned the car, he dusted off the hood of the Chevy Impala he'd crouched behind.

"How about we talk about jewelry," Troy Simms said. "You know, man, the kind where you work. You know, think about doing a favor?"

"I'm not into favors, man. I don't know nothing about Topper's inventory."

"So what could I do for you?" Troy said.

"I operate solo, man. I mean, I work my jobs, look after my mama, look after my girl. Keep low, you know."

"We can help you figure it out."

"I don't have much time to figure out anything," Alphonso said.

"Everybody's got time. Especially you."

"I don't know."

It was obvious to Troy Simms that Alphonso was stonewalling wanting to know any more about a so-called Simms plan. It couldn't be good, Alphonso thought. They were young members of The Black Panther Party and residents in west Bedlam knew that. There were times when even Troy and Terence Simms carried grocery bags for elderly residents coming out of the large Kroger store that bordered west and north

Bedlam.

Alphonso felt uneasy. He felt downright queasy. Had Troy Simms suggested that he could be an asset to the Simms brothers and their friends' so-called harmless visit to Topper's Jewelry just before closing time, and when Alphonso and Emerald Key were both present? Had Troy Simms really claimed how one ring or necklace could benefit "a larger picture of financial help," which were Troy's words? Would either of the Simms brothers or Hugh Willie be so cocky and devious as to steal a diamond ring? And that would be all. He - Troy Simms - and anyone shadowing him would be finished. Completion. Never to set foot near the jewelry store again.

Alphonso decided he was out of this picture of a catastrophe waiting to happen, if it was intended to happen.

"By the way," Troy Simms said, "pay no attention to that white boy cutting grass. I see you like looking that way at him. He works for someone else. You didn't see that boy with us last week, remember that. You didn't witness him or us, remember that."

***

ALPHONSO COULDN'T HANDLE SUCH DISTRACTIONS.

He watched his girlfriend, Fortunate, spend more

time clocking in overtime at the Empire warehouse; after work, spending more and more time in the gym, practicing cheerleading routines, and calling him at night well past eleven o'clock. She knew the ringing phone would wake his sick mother, who still nursed an upset stomach, a headache, and frequent bouts of nausea. When his mother's sister, a nurse, came over to take his mother's blood pressure, she said to Alphonso's mother, "You need to get this blood pressure down right now, sister. Go see a doctor."

Alphonso also knew Emerald Key was disappointed that he spoke to Hugh Willie in Topper's Jewelry store, not even two weeks after Willie was fired. Alphonso had damaged his image and he hadn't planned on it or anticipated the moment. He had no idea Hugh Willie had worked at Topper's. He had no idea Hugh Willie would surface in his daily routine at the store.

It was cooler outside tonight, the August humidity having surrendered its death-grip on Bedlam. Cool enough to comfort Alphonso's major distractions. Cool enough to send him shuffling to his mother's restful porch, pull up a lawn chair and a soft stool, and go to sleep right there under the stars.

All these dizzying thoughts left the jewelry store assistant's mind like the cool breeze pinning him to dream after dream, darting past him, and then leaving him inside the empty night.

DIVA

ALPHONSO COULD NOT IMAGINE THE smell of Kools cigarette smoke getting any worse.

The smoke inside Rufus T. Jones' 1967 Chevy Bonneville deepened. The ashtray overflowed. Back on Auburn Street, where Fortunate Jones lived, Rufus had whispered through the cigarette smoke, " 'Phonso, man, hop in. We going out to eat. It's cool, man."

Alphonso had dropped off Fortunate after her sixth cheerleading practice of the week, and it was only Wednesday. He barely saw her these early August days. The cheerleading squad was preparing for football season. And Alphonso was alone with Rufus T. Jones after Fortunate had gone inside to rest.

On the street, nearing evening, it was Alphonso and his girlfriend's estranged, unpredictable father. The man could get uptight in an instant, too. Alphonso knew to stare straight ahead and out the windshield. Don't look to the left. Suck in that smoke. Don't

41

complain and don't ask questions. Leave the window down until told otherwise.

Rufus pulled into the Barbecue Pit parking lot. The two savored ribs, corn-on-the-cob, stewed tomatoes, red beans and rice. Rufus deliberately ate fast, laying his fork and knife on the plate before Alphonso could butter his bread. He was down to some sort of business. He brought up hubcaps without venturing into other small talk.

No matter how casually Rufus elaborated on the subject of the hubcaps in his garage, and no matter how convincing Rufus became on why hubcaps mattered to the American automobile industry, Alphonso acted like he had never once peered into Rufus' garage. He winced only once under the umbrella of cigarette smoke in the restaurant. He slid sideway in his booth, turning a shoulder toward other tables.

Rufus tried to convince Alphonso that he could make ten dollars for each sale of a hubcap. He was willing to make Alphonso a partner. He twirled a toothpick between his teeth waiting for Alphonso to finish his corn and rice. Alphonso said, "No."

"I'd disappoint my mama. Not the work I want, Mr. Jones."

"People's hubcaps fall off, 'Phonso. See that? They get all loose and all warped, scratched up on these streets," Rufus said. "People need new ones. That's where I come in. We, I mean. We get new ones."

"You stealing?"

"Naw, young man. I replenish supplies. I keep them hubcaps moving in the right direction, toward helpless people."

This didn't appease Alphonso whatsoever, and it must not have escaped Rufus' demeanor, because he drove back to Bedlam in silence, blowing smoke with sighs, letting Alphonso out by the curb, two full blocks from his house.

Before he let Alphonso out, Rufus Jones perked up. He launched into a blunt interrogation: "You ain't planning on mentioning this dinner to Fortunate, paid by me?"

"No way. I say nothing."

"If a Bedlam cop comes up, says 'Where's Fortunate Jones,' you know nothing, right?"

"Yeah. Got that, Mr. Jones. Not my business. I just say she's a cheerleader and gets straight-A's."

Fortunate Jones' father drove off, with that gray Bonneville exhaust lining the street.

***

EMERALD KEY, THAT DAY, HAD talked so much cheerleading to Alphonso that the only image in his mind was losing his own girlfriend to this sport.

They cleaned a new dusty display case for jewelry

43

that came in a gigantic wooden crate. And Emerald talked. They wheeled the case to yet another corner of the jewelry store. She continued to talk.

"You know," Emerald said, "a girl on our team, us cheerleaders, you know she steals boyfriends. She's after Sheila Dalryple's boyfriend. You know him? Clark Wright? Drives a Camaro like he's a king? His father is rich, too. Clark is just stupid. He's always been slow-headed, since kindergarten."

"Nope. I don't see him."

Emerald launched into a tirade about this boy Clark's ignorant side and his unwillingness to see Sheila's valuable raw feelings. Alphonso felt for Sheila Dalryple, too. He didn't condone this boy's behavior, his lack of loyalty and the two-timing on Sheila. He would never do that to Fortunate. Emerald Key was a young pretty woman. Tall, yet very cute, in Alphonso's opinion. A real talker, too much so, but humorous and charming and in control of her job tasks, like Fortunate Jones.

Emerald lived three houses around the corner from Bettman's Grocery in west Bedlam. Alphonso had tended to notice her occasionally when he worked for old man Bettman.

If he wanted, Alphonso thought, he could try to ask Emerald for a modest kiss, or at least to hold her hand when he walked her to the car. But, he'd never do that behind Fortunate's back, and he was confident, anyway, that Emerald would land a boyfriend once school officially started in a few weeks.

Still, the more Emerald talked about the absurd politics of cheerleading and the favoritism the coach showed toward two new freshmen, the longer it took for Alphonso to tell Emerald that he planned to quit the jewelry store. This was his last day. He had not revealed this to her earlier. He was almost too ashamed, since she was so patient and dutiful to teach him the sensitive skills behind dealing with customers and handling jewelry at the end of the day. He would tell Dick Topper today; it was time that Topper know the truth.

Alphonso was unnerved more each day not knowing how Fortunate really felt about him. With her work at the Empire and her cheerleading, she was missing in his life. He just wanted one evening alone with her. Inexcusably alone. Romantically alone. Alone in a place where he could give her an extended hug. Where they could smooch. Where he wouldn't hear the words, "I have to go to work."

Was that too much to ask?

The only solution was to take a job sweeping floors at the Empire warehouse, where he could be as close to her as he was to Emerald Key in Topper's Jewelry. He would pursue that option as soon as he got a final paycheck from Dick Topper.

The store owner stepped out of his office still

wearing his jeweler's eyeglass, which could enlarge the tiniest of gemstones for his eyes to examine. The better to set or clean the most intricate diamonds. Topper could have heard Emerald Key berate a co-cheerleader. He could have heard her exclaim, "Thief. Girl-stealing boy-thief witch." Those were powerful words, and they rose and planted themselves across the back of the store. Those were words Topper might take seriously in a place of lofty business.

Alphonso walked his boss back into his office. "Mr. Topper, a word with you."

Topper took off his jeweler's eyeglass. It had the thick lens of a microscope. He sat down not in his desk chair, but on top of his messy desk, kicking out his legs as if exercising.

"Mr. Topper, I need to leave the store. For good. I like it, but it's not for me."

"I was getting concerned about you. You've been droopy lately."

"I ain't myself."

"You come back if you change you your mind. I understand change. You kids change like the wind. Except Emerald. She's solid. She has a key to the store."

"Hate that I let you down," Alphonso said.

"No," Topper said. "I just want you to touch base with me if you hear of or see anyone snooping. I'll get another hand to help Tamara."

Alphonso flipped his store badge with his name inscribed on it on Dick Topper's desk. When he walked out the door, the door chime, for some reason, sounded like a clock chiming, another hour ticking by. The hours were piling up on Alphonso. The days hurried by. They dragged Alphonso along with them. He had no chance but to carefully count those days, those hours blinding him to what exactly he wanted to say to Fortunate Jones.

FIND

HE WAS GOING TO FIND his girl.

Alphonso's girlfriend nearly ran one third of the Empire warehouse. Her floor supervisor, a cross-eyed old man named Joe, let her decide where to place smaller equipment in the warehouse like racks or shelving on which to stack light and heavy tools. Joe gave her that authority. Joe entrusted her with cutting tools. She even used a jigsaw to perfection once, cutting a two-by-twelve board into three even pieces.

When school started in a month, she would have to trim her hours to ten a week. Joe understood that, which was why he was working her mercilessly now.

Alphonso was looking for Fortunate as he mopped a tile floor in the lunchroom. He looked out the window into the center of the warehouse. Fortunate's supervisor let her add and subtract the numbers of inventory equipment in her half of the warehouse. She was only part-time and a senior Honor Society student

48

at Bedlam High. Cross-eyed Joe trusted her with money. He allowed Fortunate to take any checks that came in after six o'clock to the bank the next morning, saving his secretary from the hassle of hurrying to the bank and straight to work.

Cross-eyed Joe had interviewed Alphonso and hired him to move cartons, crates, and cables from one end of the warehouse to the other. Alphonso had to move them by hand or with a portable hand-cart. He was in no way given the liberty of driving the lone forklift that was operated by a woman who had worked at the Empire for twenty-two years. She was already busy in her own little sphere of the warehouse.

Alphonso needed a paycheck, sure. It was 1967, he played no sports and no musical instruments. He was handsome and tall, and he combed his impressive, spiked afro every time he got a chance. A paycheck was always a nice dream, in spite of the fact he actually did work. He was just particular with his job-seeking. In this way he was much like any late-teen boy at a working age. At Bettman's Grocery, he liked candy and sandwich meat, so working for old man Bettman, before he got fired, was a priority. Still, there was only one girl he wanted to impress. A paycheck he could use, sure, but he landed this warehouse job over brushing cobwebs off windows at a ritzy jewelry store because he could see Fortunate Jones during the afternoon, at least until school and football games started. Then her cheerleading would really reach a pinnacle. Inside Topper's Jewelry story and against the cobwebs and dust pans and glamorous, two, jewelry display cases, Fortunate did not exist.

She existed here, inside the Empire. She was a young, black female leader among a mix of white and black men and several women. The women sewed canvases, stacked sheets of drywall in bins upon their delivery, and fixed equipment.

Alphonso now pushed a broom toward Fortunate. She cautioned him not to spend much time near her. No place to play a romantic interlude.

"We on tonight?" he said.

"I got cheerleading at seven. I'll be home at ten."

"You can't miss one practice? That's eight in a row."

"Some of us are trying out for captain and co-captain. It's deep."

"You know I miss you," he said.

"I miss you, too, but you know how things are. I'm trying to get ahead. Be someone. Everything counts toward the future. That's what Home Economics was for."

"Cheerleading is just school, girl. It ain't ahead. Counting sheets of drywall ain't ahead."

"It's about image and being involved. You should be like that. You tall. You can play ball. You'd start varsity if you tried out. Do what you want. You stay with me, you get somewhere."

"I'll get a paycheck."

And maybe he would do what she said. Maybe he would stay close to Fortunate. Maybe he would not drop out of Bedlam like he planned to do in a month. He was nice enough, but not companionable. He didn't view himself as a team player. He found it strenuous to socialize. He played favorites. He had four or five. Fortunate Jones was Alphonso's best friend, although he realized Sheila Dalryple was likely Fortunate's best friend. He could live with that.

He could not live with the belief that it would suit him to mostly see her at the Empire. This likely would not work for him.. He needed to see Fortunate at other times. She often angered him enough by not being able to see him that he basically didn't care if he quit school. He wanted to be visible, but not as visible as a cheerleader.

He was going to find himself, like that 1963 Bob Dylan song he'd heard emphasized. He thought about those Dylan lyrics:"How many years can some people exist, before they're allowed to be free?"

***

HIS MOTHER'S BLOUSE, FULLY UNBUTTONED, still hadn't helped her solve her problem of groping for oxygen, for full breaths.

Alphonso's mind collected these dispassionate images of his mother in their house as much as it tried to coax him toward her on the floor. Or coax him toward the telephone. He didn't know what to do. It was his mother lying next to the coffee table. Alphonso kept stumbling. He tried to speak but couldn't.

When he did gain his balance and move, it was with blistering speed. His wallet and keys fell out of his back pocket, keys rattling on the floor. He struggled to stay upright and move. His cry of "mama" went unheard.

Her two shoes were scattered across the living room. One couch cushion turned over. Newspaper pages in disarray. An ashtray nearly scooted off the coffee table. She had probably gasped for air. She obviously couldn't make it to the telephone. Her right leg seemed cocked in the direction of the phone in the hallway.

Again, Alphonso observed, with ear to her chest, she was not breathing. Not capable of a breath. What was he to do? He didn't know CPR. But, pulling her blouse together, he knew how to bury his head on her mid-section. He kept his head there over a minute - at least. His ear seemed glued to her mid-section, and still she didn't move.

He crawled to the phone in the hallway and next to the kitchen. The last thing he wanted to do was call the police. But he called. He asked for an ambulance. He said to the police desk receptionist: "I came in from work at the Empire, and she laying there on the floor having fallen off the couch, not moving. My mama. She's on the floor. Her eyes tilted back in her head. I don't know what to do. I ain't thinking right."

When the two policemen arrived, they walked through the open front door without knocking. They moved out of the way for two paramedics. When they found Alphonso, he, too, was curled on the floor, hugging the phone still not returned to its cradle.

MIRACLE

IT WAS A MIRACLE THAT Alphonso sat sad yet bewildered in Snookies Restaurant and saw an odd sequence of activity occurring in Topper's Jewelry.

It had been two weeks since his mother died and he witnessed her burial. Two weeks since his uncle, who was his mother's favorite brother, sat next to him on the funeral home's lumpy couch, and vowed that he would have a place for his nephew at his house. Alphonso's uncle, a trumpet player and machine shop laborer with only one healthy-working eye, lived two blocks from his deceased sister. His name was Henry Weasel, although family and friends called him "Pop," or sometimes "Seeing Eye."

At Snookies, Alphonso sat alone in a booth by the window facing Cooper Avenue. He could see the tall figure of Emerald Key moving from behind the display counter to get closer to four unusual-looking customers. It only took a moment for Alphonso to recognize three: Troy and Terence Simms and Hugh Willie. He squinted trying to place the other white guy accompanying them. He had straight hair which hung down and curled above his eyes. Emerald kept busy speaking to each one as if she was denying them access to look at jewelry.

A waitress brought Alphonso his cheeseburger, fries, and applesauce, and forgot his large iced tea. When she brought it after three long minutes, she noticed Alphonso had not touched his burger. She noticed him staring at Topper's. She took the initiative to set the iced tea even closer to his arm, which, too, had not moved in over five minutes. She tapped the cold glass of tea against his arm in jest, still not cajoling him from his observation. She shook her head, choosing not to further disrupt his obvious daydreaming or at least his keen interest in a window full of necklaces and bracelets.

Alphonso smelled fries cooking in the vat of hot oil behind the counter, only to be overtaken by the smell of onions wafting across the one room of tables and booths. No measure of grease or burnt-toasted buns could distract him from his view of Topper's. He watched Dick Topper stand in for Emerald. He talked to the guys while Emerald bit a fingernail. There was little movement except for Topper's hands. He seemed to be pointing out certain pieces of jewelry in the process of answering lame questions. Topper stood nervously bouncing on his feet.

Alphonso watched Hugh Willie walk by himself to another display case. Emerald's eyes followed him. In less than two minutes, Hugh Willie was out of sight. Emerald disappeared to the back. After a few minutes, Hugh Willie rejoined the group, and now Troy Simms, the talker, separated himself. He stood five feet away from Dick Topper, bending over a display case and gawking closely at rings. Alphonso knew those display cases well.

The waitress passed by, said, "Excuse me? Your food okay?"

"Cool. Real good." Alphonso had eaten one fry and taken one bite of his cold cheeseburger. He took another bite in front of the waitress. In five more minutes, he'd eaten half the burger. He also watched Elmer "Breezy" Klump pull his cop cruiser in front of the jewelry store. Breezy flicked ashes from his cigarettes out the window. He stared into the store without getting out. The only question that lingered in Alphonso's mind was, "What are you guys really doing in Topper's? You're not looking for a job."

Alphonso shifted his legs in a failed, feckless attempt to rise from his booth and walk over to the store. At the very least, he could possibly break up the gathering by just saying, "You cats don't need to be in here. You ain't shopping." But, he grabbed his plate and pushed it away. He propped his elbows on the table and watched Breezy step out of his cruiser, stand at its side and peer with disinterest into the store, and then return to the comfort of the cruiser, and drive away.

A minute later, Troy and Terence Simms backed up toward the door waving both arms high, as if suggesting, "I have nothing, man. I'm walking out clean, no trouble intended." The pair of Hugh Willie and the other guy with floppy hair soon followed the Simms brothers. They, too, raised their arms and laughed, heading down Cooper Avenue.

AFTER NO TRACE OF THE four remained, Emerald walked out of Topper's in the direction of north Bedlam, although she lived a few blocks away in west Bedlam. Alphonso left a five dollar bill on the table, flashed a peace sign to the waitress, and shouted to Emerald once outside Snookies: "Emerald, you, hey, come over here, hurry."

She spun around and hurried across the street.

"You in Snookies a long time?" she said. "We had an event."

"I saw. I mean, I saw at the last minute," he said. "Just about ran over to Topper's, and just left my cheeseburger on the table. Here you are."

He led Emerald to his car where she said she could catch her breath. He wanted to play music on low from his car radio; Emerald reached over and turned the volume off. "You got to listen," she said.

Alphonso sat back against his driver's door and window and ran a toothpick along his front teeth. He waited for Emerald to start talking after his simple two word lead: "What happened?"

"I knew they were up to no good, which is why I called for Topper. He came right out. They were Troy and Terence Simms. Hugh Willie. That fourth boy was Wayne deLong. You know him. From Mudtown. He races his cars. Guess he's friends with Hugh. Guess they race cars together. Anyway, Hugh wanders over to a case and I see where he's going. It's an empty case except for a few older necklaces. But they're pearls. Maybe Hugh Willie had a notion. Easy case to get into."

Alphonso just listened. He took a pencil out of the ashtray and scratched his scalp buried under a round afro.

"I had to convince Topper not to call the cops. I told him, 'I'm going home.' Nothing was done. They might have sized the place up, but you couldn't have anyone outright arrested. Not for not doing anything. They walked out waving their arms around like they'd pulled the joke on Topper."

"But why did I see Breezy Klump from Bedlam?" Alphonso said.

"Don't know. He was just there. Luck of the draw. He just stayed in his car. Guess he saw Topper smiling and laughing. That was his nervousness on real edge. He sweated raindrops. Back of his shirt soaking wet. Man was frightened. That's why I went in the back to call Sheila Dalryple."

"I wondered why you went to the back," he said.

"To call Sheila first. She knows Topper's brother the mayor. She can even call him by his first name, Cecil. He's always over at his brother's house next to Sheila. I wanted the mayor to do something before the Bedlam cops. Topper's brother has the ultimate power. He could've had more than Breezy Klump to show up. And the mayor would have showed up, too. Scared those boys to death. Probably had them arrested for loitering."

"So Sheila didn't call the mayor?"

"She called your girlfriend Fortunate."

"Why her?" Alphonso said, dropping his pencil. He sat up and straightened his back, his elbow on the steering wheel.

"She was home. But she was headed for work She called me at Topper's. She said, 'Where's Alphonso?' And I said, 'Who knows? I thought you knew.'"

"Was Fortunate gonna come over anyway?" Alphonso said.

"Nope. She just said for me to go in and tell Troy Simms, 'If you don't leave in one minute with Hugh Willie, I'm going to call the cops.' And Fortunate said I should look at my watch and count the seconds the whole time. Stare them down. Give them the evil eye. Force them out. Show them that I, instead of Dick Topper, was in charge. Make them run for the door."

"So, Fortunate had it right. You could threaten those guys instead of Topper."

"Here's the last thing that I argued with Topper about. Topper said, 'I know someone stole a ring.' He said, 'I can see it missing from the case.' I said, 'No, Mr. Topper, I took that one ring back to clean. A customer wanted it cleaned before buying it, and you weren't here. It's on your desk.' He said, 'I don't think so. It's been stolen.' I said, 'No, none of those guys got it when you weren't looking.' He said, 'Hugh Willie? Wasn't Hugh Willie eyeballing that ring?' I told Topper, 'No. Willie was just being his slow, follow-the-leader self. Hugh Willie just stood around bored.' Topper said, 'What about those other guys? One of them wandered toward that case.' And I said, 'No, sir. I know where that ring is.' I checked quickly all around the display cases before I left, and I needed to leave. No sign of theft. Topper still is unconvinced. He says, 'I need to see that ring.' I showed him a ring from the back, and he says, 'That's not it. Not the one I'm talking about.' So, I don't think he even knows anything."

"You think one of the Simms brothers stole a ring?" Alphonso said.

"No way. I could spot where they were the whole

time, even if Topper, who's half-blind and so short, couldn't see a thing. He wouldn't see a bat flitting around the store."

It was getting stuffy in the car. Alphonso drove Emerald home.

GONE

ALWAYS A GENTLEMAN AROUND FORTUNATE, Alphonso opened his car door for her and let her find the radio station she wanted to play. Fortunate was in the mood for jazz, so she spun the AM-dial to WNOP, the Jazz Ark.

She could walk to work at the Empire warehouse, although Alphonso volunteered to drive her today. It was raining. He'd led her to the car holding an umbrella over her head. When he drove through the heart of west Bedlam, he slowed down upon seeing a Bedlam police car outside of Topper's Jewelry. He pulled over. The store's window front was shielded from the rain by a cloth awning, and Alphonso could see through the glass that officer Breezy was talking to Dick Topper. He wondered what that was about.

He was far too curious. He parked in front of Snookie's behind a food delivery truck and entering Topper's, he ignored raindrops sliding down his cheek.

Dick Topper and Breezy Klump looked at him with disbelief and paused their conversation. Topper had escorted Breezy around the display case from which claimed a ring had vanished.

"Alphonso?" Topper said, as if addressing a stranger.

"Just passing by. Want to say thanks for that last check," Alphonso said. "Fortunate got it to me. You saved a stamp."

"Right."

"Son," Klump said, "Funny you're here. Mr. Topper here had said you were a loyal watcher-outer for a slew of guys hanging around his store."

"Not really. I mostly kept things clean."

"You know anyone who was in this store that day?" Topper jumped in. "I'm sure Emerald filled you in. And she's tight-lipped because she swears nothing is missing, and she's beyond discussing it."

"No sir," he said.

"Not at all?" Klump said.

"No sir."

"Just remember, I wouldn't hold back even one crumb of information."

"We sold that ring a while back," Alphonso said.

"I don't agree with that, but I won't argue," Topper said. "I'm heated as it is."

"Young man, you know something we don't?" Klump said. It was as if the officer hadn't heard a word of Alphonso's explanation.

"My friend Emerald knows it sold. Look it up in the books."

"You seem pretty confident," Klump said.

They all moved toward the door. Before Topper could put on a straw hat, activate the alarm, and lock the front door, Alphonso hopped in his car, gazed straight ahead, and began driving his girlfriend to the Empire.

He thought how he could have suggested that Klump talk to any of the three guys he'd come into contact with: the Simms brothers and Hugh Willie. As he drove, the image of one polished hubcap lying on the floor of Rufus Jones' garage planted itself in his mind. For all he imagined, that hubcap could have been an expensive ring.

Alphonso could have said to Klump or Dick Topper that any one of those three were odd ones to be in any jewelry store. He'd chosen not to snitch. He had no proof of theft anyway. Those guys were showing they could act intimidatingly in a small store. Alphonso thought, "I don't know if Emerald lost count of the rings, or if one did get snatched. But she acts like she knows everything."

He felt a lump in his throat. At one time that day, as he sat in Snookies nibbling his fries, there was tense commotion in the jewelry store, a degree of uncertain movement. He couldn't see everything. So, who could be sure?

He dropped off Fortunate and went back to his house. Before he started to pack two suitcases in preparation for his move to the Weasel's home, Alphonso headed right toward the refrigerator.

He had always heard his mother say, "If you need cash in an emergency, and only in an emergency, look in the back of the refrigerator inside that empty carton of eggs, and you'll find cash. Not much, but it's there. Don't touch it otherwise." His mother had made so many trips with her then-boyfriend to join protests in Chicago or Detroit or Cleveland that she became adamant about leaving some cash for her son, although he held a job. Alphonso's mother kept tucking cash in the egg carton for him, after all. She hadn't touched it either.

Alphonso had trouble deciding what she meant by "emergency." It was his call. He could be low on gas. He might need to buy Fortunate one rose. He might need to restock his candy supply from Bettman's. He might need some new shoes. He had no idea what kind of emergency she dreamed. It was a safe place, the empty egg carton. Who ate eggs in his household? No one. He and his mother both despised eggs.

He opened the egg carton and cash fell out. He sorted through the bills on the kitchen floor, in the growing dusk with the curtains closed, the lights out, the doors locked, and the refrigerator door still open, shedding light on the cash. He tried not to look around because he still shook every time he thought terribly long about his mother. His arms twitched. He couldn't count adequately; he kept starting over: "Five, ten, thirty, fifty," he recited aloud. Wads of five and one dollar bills. At least his mother had thought of him. He crammed all fifty dollars in his pocket and remembered he had forty in his wallet. He found a single white envelope in a kitchen drawer.

For now, this was all he needed. The envelope would be in someone else's hands soon.

***

IN THE LATE EVENING, ALPHONSO took a serious chance: he drove by himself to Dick Topper's house in north Bedlam. It was now dark at ten p.m. He drove intentionally at this time of night. He knew there was a slight chance he would be spotted walking up on the Topper porch. He also knew Topper was probably in bed. But, he remained steadfast with his plan, and he had the money to pull it off.

Alphonso initially thought he'd park on the street outside of Sheila Dalryple's house, though he changed his mind as he turned onto her and Topper's street. He saw the Dalryple's porchlight turned on, so he decided not to park in front of Sheila's house. Anyway, it could look suspicious. There were perhaps a few neighbors

66

who might recognize his polished Ford Galaxy, especially the tires' white-walls, and there were those who might draw a mental line from a boy parking his car to his interest in visiting a girl – Sheila Dalryple – late in the evening. Which meant, to Alphonso, that a nosy neighbor might think a young black guy was too overly eager to visit Sheila Dalryple, which was as far from reality as it could be.

Alphonso's mind was overactive. He just wanted to drop off an envelope and get going.

He wanted to spend minimal time alone in north Bedlam.

He wanted to drop his envelope containing fifty dollars in the Topper family mailbox and comfortably drive home realizing that he had done a good deed. An anonymous good deed. Topper would never know. Topper would never know that this envelope money came originally from his mother saving "emergency cash" for Alphonso. He had written "For Dick Topper" in large black letters on the envelope, and yet Topper would never know who stashed fifty bucks in the envelope. He could never decipher that handwriting. Impossible. He'd never once seen Alphonso's handwriting.

Dick Topper did not need fifty bucks from Alphonso Peace. Yet Alphonso kept trying to rearrange the real guilt he was feeling into a far corner of his conscience over the fact that maybe – just maybe – a ring was stolen. Maybe he and Emerald were wrong. He felt sorry for Dick Topper. Alphonso thought he could have come out of Snookies Restaurant a lot sooner and disrupted the moment when the Simms brothers, Hugh Willie, and Wayne deLong entered Topper's. Topper had hired Alphonso on several fair conditions. Alphonso got paid. Dick Topper trusted him around the jewelry. In less than four weeks, Emerald Key had taught him much about the jewelry business.

Alphonso just couldn't be sure about the ring. He no longer worked for Topper, but still he felt like he had personal stake in the appearance of the store. He had trusted Emerald's judgment; she knew every piece of jewelry in every case, in every box, and in the backroom vault across from Topper's desk. She swore not one ring was missing.

What if, out of uncustomary negligence, Emerald was wrong? What if she missed knowing about one ring, the diamond ring Topper swore was missing? What if she missed her count by one? All in all, Alphonso sided with Emerald's judgment. She acted most of the time as if she co-owned the store. Topper could always be erratic and a dreamer.

He pulled the Galaxy under the big tree that Owl the cat had climbed. The oak branches were so long and dense that they hung perfectly across part of the street. At night, any car was partially hidden under them. He trotted up the Topper walkway and onto the porch and tossed the sealed envelope in the mail slot. He'd kept the Galaxy's engine running. No one, as far as he could see, was sitting on his or her porch this late at ten-thirty.

It was still drizzling. Alphonso parked outside of the Empire, waited for Fortunate to finish her late shift. Leaving work, she wouldn't miss his car sitting outside the warehouse.

She was so tired she immediately curled up her legs on the wide front seat and laid her head on Alphonso's thigh while he drove her home. He let his girlfriend lean a good deal on him, walking her to her front door. "Good night, sweetness," he said. "I'll be at my uncle's by tomorrow."

He finished packing his suitcases yet left so many shirts lying on his bed. He'd come back later. With his uncle's house a few blocks away, he decided to take in the night air and tote his two suitcases up the street. He locked his car doors. He'd come back for his car tomorrow. Those two suitcases had been his grandfather's and the musty smell trailed Alphonso wherever he walked.

He gripped the suitcases with the same command with which he'd carried the envelope up to Dick Topper's mailbox. He never looked back toward his mother's street. It seemed like the drizzling rain had stopped, yet he still sidestepped puddles, careful not to get his gym shoes muddy. He was going to be stepping into a new home.

Lost in thought the way he was, he trusted he would see a porchlight on waiting for him. In this outpouring of night all the sudden, it would be the last light   he'd   know   tonight.

Action Steps

Reviews from readers like you play a huge part in helping me spread the word about my fiction.

If you liked the novella, please consider taking a few minutes to leave a review on Amazon, Goodreads, Facebook, or Twitter. But, especially Amazon. I greatly appreciate your time and your kind words.

Keep up with the publications of the next Shine in Bedlam novels. Sign up for my email mailing list at www.jeffreyhillard.com. On the site, I have a free copy of a short ebook on writing creatively that I wrote, and I want you to have it for signing up.

Expect to read future novels, novellas, and short stories in the Shine in Bedlam YA series.

Jeffrey Hillard
Cincinnati, Ohio

A Note from the Author

The following print and visual works were invaluable resources in my writing this novella. They proved indispensable in providing a far deeper understanding of the 1960s, and they enriched my vision for the novel: The 60s: The Story of a Decade by The New Yorker Magazine (Henry Finder, editor); The Age of Great Dreams: America in the 1960s (American Century Series) by David Farber; Black Panthers: Vanguard of the Revolution (Stanley Nelson, Director).

Acknowledgments

I owe a debt of gratitude to the following for their generous help in making the publication of this novel possible. Their talents and insights are boundless. Their presence in my writing life, priceless. Thank you: Brenda Elam-Huff, Chelsea Hillard, Betty C. Hillard, Tracc Conger, Jennifer Holbrock, Jacqui Slabach, and Elizabeth Barkley. Special thanks to Dr. H. James Williams, president of Mount St. Joseph University, to my colleagues at Mount St. Joseph University, to the entire Mount community, and to The Public Library of Cincinnati and Hamilton County.

I am so grateful to the following friends, colleagues, and family members for their support of my work over the years. Many thanks to Thom Atkinson, John Ballard, Robert Bodle, S. Mary Bookser, Mary Ann Edwards, Larry Gartner, Karen George, Susan Glassmeyer, Tom Groh, Christine Grote, Randy Haight, the late William C. Hillard, Caron Hofer, Wayne Hofer, Jon Hughes, Susan Hughes, Paul Jenkins, Jerry Judge, Steve Kissing, Carol Feiser Laque, Craig Lloyd, Tim Lynch, Elizabeth Mason, Jennifer Morris, Robert Murphy, Ryck Neube, Kathleen Owens, Barbara Petersen, Eddie Reeb, Rebecca Reeb, Peter Robinson, William Schutzius, Bob Shacochis, Drew Shannon, Charlie Skillman, Michael Sontag, Tom Watts, and Karl Zuelke. Thanks also to the members of Cincinnati Writers' Project and the Greater Cincinnati Writers League.

About the Author

Jeffrey Hillard is an award-winning writer and teacher. He is the author of four books of poems, two novels, a chapbook of short stories, and a book of non-fiction. The Alphonso Rap is part of the Shine in Bedlam YA/Adult series. In addition to working as a former publisher, editor, anthology co-editor, and literary advocate for over 30 years, Mr. Hillard also taught writing and mentored individuals in incarceration facilities in the 2000s. Among his numerous awards, in 2015-2016, he worked as Writer-in-Residence for The Public Library of Cincinnati and Hamilton County. He teaches writing and literature at Mount St. Joseph University in Cincinnati, Ohio, where in 2019 he received the university's Distinguished Scholar Award.

Visit online at:

www.jeffreyhillard.com
www.facebook.com/jeffrey.hillard.9
www.twitter.com/JSHillard (@JSHillard)

Read an excerpt from the Shine in Bedlam novel *Shine in Grit City*

If you enjoyed *The Alphonso Rap*, here is part of Chapter One of the new novel in the series.

Chapter One - **ENCASED**

HE WALKED WITH A PLAN.

No. It was more that he walked with a need to accomplish.

Or else it was with a sense of hope. Big hope. Maybe his hope was misplaced. Maybe he walked not realizing he was definitely alone on these train tracks.

Shine Ross felt the September light mist gather around the tracks. He didn't have a raincoat and he didn't care. The mist seemed to ease when he got off his bike. Two or three stars had given way to cloud cover this early morning, and while Shine walked along the tracks on the far south end of Bedlam, he watched the sky, looking for JoJo the parrot. He turned his head and turned it again. He stared into the trees. He tried hard to stare into every dark crevice of thin branches.

This was the last time. This would be the last walk in which he'd think JoJo the parrot might appear in a tree.

JoJo was gone.

The Amazon parrot, owned by Shine's Uncle Jerry and Aunt Ruth had escaped at the beginning of summer. By now, JoJo might be swooping along the Ozarks, on his way to finding Arizona. Shine had spent his summer of 1968 dodging toys in backyards and elbowing his way through vines in Garland Park, running after JoJo, tracking the parrot when sightings occurred.

It took many days after Shine last saw and chased after JoJo near Garland Park, near his house in north Bedlam, to finally believe his Uncle Jerry's notion that JoJo was now flying west toward a migrant community of lost parrots in the American southwest, toward a warmer climate. Uncle Jerry had tried to calm Shine's sense of defeat upon realizing JoJo would probably not return. Jerry talked to him about regions out west where parrots gathered in communities and generated their parrot families. Shine's uncle had read about this phenomenon in a nature magazine. There were photographs of the migrations, of parrot communities, and of their gorgeous feathers and crowns.

For Shine, no more searching for JoJo after today. This would be it.

No more fake promises to himself that he would find and catch the bird. Losing the bird was a disastrous accident.

It was an easy attempt to transport the caged parrot into the backseat of uncle Jerry's 1967 Pontiac Bonneville, a gigantic car, but it became a botched attempt at handling the vast size of the cage.

Shine had been parrot-sitting. After returning from a short vacation, and after picking up JoJo, Jerry banged JoJo's cage against his Bonneville. The cage caught an open door. The awkward collision triggered the bottom to open, setting JoJo free. It flew toward neighbors' tree-lined backyards.

JoJo clung to those backyards in north Bedlam. He perched on his first outdoor bird feeder.

Shine worried so much that he couldn't sleep: nightmares, an upset stomach. He tried to focus on playing basketball and his trumpet and hopping a few trains with Moondog. When he worked a few hours a week at the recreation shelter, he'd wander over to the creek and search for JoJo in trees.

The year of 1968 had been gruesome enough with the murders of Martin Luther King in April and Presidential candidate, Bobby Kennedy, in July, and the hostile war in South Vietnam, with American soldiers heading deeper and deeper into a jungle seething with enemy attacks.

Everyone in Shine's family believed that JoJo had flown away.

That last time Shine tried to rescue the parrot, a boy ran toward him so excited that his shouting fractured the moment of near-capture. Shine was in a tree coaxing JoJo to come closer. He had a light blanket ready to toss over the bird. The boy's shriek's scared JoJo and off the bird flew. Shine sprinted down the treeline. Others followed. They followed JoJo from tree to tree. Until the parrot flew off and definitely away from the woods.

NOW, HE WALKED DOWN A railroad track he was not familiar with.

He walked with his bike at his side. Something about the perfect linear construction of a railroad track held him spellbound.

He'd hopped trains with Moondog over the summer. They only had two accidents. Moondog once twisted his ankle hopping off, and once they hopped one boxcar too late in the afternoon. Dusk sneaked into a cornfield they walked through. Soon, with the increasing darkness, it seemed the cornstalks were vanishing in front of them. An occasional streetlight escorted them to a pay phone in a little town where Shine continually clenched his teeth, knowing he was going to plead with his mother to come get them.

They also met a hobo who projected the American freedom and American ingenuity of living with hardly *anything*, which kept Shine thinking about the hobo most of the summer. Shine feared that lifestyle. He feared the idea of owning nothing. Which is exactly why he considered that hobo one of the most amazing people he'd ever met.

Shine still thought of this year's newest assassination that had gone down a little over a month ago: Robert F. Kennedy, in California, in a hotel kitchen pantry in the early morning after a speech. 1968 so far: The year of trauma. The escalation of war and of totally blunt television footage of people protesting the ongoing Vietnam War on main streets in Chicago,, Washington, New York, Oakland, Los Angeles.

Shine couldn't sleep the night before he got on his bike and rode over to these tracks.

He fought off a recurring dream of JoJo flying around Bedlam, flapping his wings above his parents' house, landing on his windowsill, staring in the window, and watching Shine sleep.

The dreams woke him every hour. He got up and splashed cold water on his face. He massaged his eyelids. He clipped his fingernails. He flushed the toilet in the middle of the night. He splashed more water. He relied on cold water to clip JoJo from his dream world.

It didn't work.

In these dreams, he also saw JoJo darting from tree to tree, a short distance from north Bedlam where he lived. It had to be somewhere around south Bedlam. Not west Bedlam, the largely black Bedlam neighborhood. West Bedlam was where his best friend, Moondog Weasel, lived. It was the neighborhood of his mentor, "Pop" Weasel, Moondog's father and the constant influence of Shine's trumpet-playing.

JoJo was nowhere near the high school in north Bedlam, a short walk from Shine's house. The parrot was nowhere near the high school in north Bedlam, a short walk from Shine's house. The parrot was nowhere near Garland Park, two minutes from his house, the long stretch of woods where he last saw JoJo.

SHINE BELIEVED THAT ONE OF his dreams had been shaped by an image of Lefty's Tavern.

In the Bedlam community of Mudtown, Lefty's sat near another set of railroad tracks. Bedlam was mostly bordered by tracks and by one long fence. The fence stretched from one side of the city and formed a kind of border between it and the city of Jefferson Heights.

About four or five very long streets with small houses squeezed together made up Mudtown. In his dream, Shine remembered JoJo flying past Lefty's. It was a dream, afterall. The brick tavern acting as a gateway to another little suburb just after these railroad tracks, Lefty's sat in a far corner of Mudtown. Shine remembered seeing the tavern's Hudepohl Beer sign lighting a window. He remembered a mild wind brushing against the metal outdoor Schlitz Beer sign, causing it to sway.

Since Shine couldn't sleep, he got up at six-thirty in the morning, brushed his teeth, pushed his bike out of the garage, and peddled toward Mudtown. He was oblivious of some men walking toward their seven-to-three shifts at the mattress and paper-cutting factories. He was oblivious to men carrying their lunchboxes toward the tool-and-die factory and to men in their cars speeding down the two or three busy streets to get to their preferred parking spots.

Shine's thinking wavered so much around JoJo the Amazon parrot's flight west. When his Uncle Jerry told him about the story of lost parrots migrating to Arizona, Shine couldn't believe a bird could fly that far.

He felt with his hand the metal Band-Aid box in a back pants pocket. It had dents in the sides. He started to take a cigarette from the box but put it back in. He wanted to pitch the box; he'd hold off just long enough to finish, at some point, the last few cigarettes. Maybe later.

AND NOW NEAR THE TRAIN track he discovered a body.

Or, he was confused: was it a human body? Was this seriously a body? What was it?

Although the mist had mostly stopped, the air was dense. Hard for Shine to clearly. He would have a hard time seeing the headlights of a coming train. The seeming body lay slumped and curled several yards away from the rails. Was it a mannequin? Was it a massive tree branch shaped like a body? Was it a cardboard box shaped like a torso, with one end shaped like a head?

Shine stared at it. He didn't move for awhile.

The quietness of the early morning on these tracks amplified the chirping of crickets. Their chirping had crept up on him. The chirping increased each step he took toward the cardboard-tree-branch-or-bodily form which, to Shine, definitely kept looking more and more like a body.

And it was.

He stood mayben fifteen feet away from it. He wouldn't go further. He detected a strange smell. It wasn't a cardboard box. He noticed black hair on a head that was turned downward. He couldn't see a face. He saw that one arm was missing. He saw dark red blood; a shirt ripped, one shoe missing. Shine took a step back, holding onto his bike, once this notion of a human being penetrated his thoughts. "Who is this?" he thought. "What am I seeing? Why here?"

Shine thought he might be in trouble for even stumbling across a body, a person. He stared. His thoughts turned onto his own participation in the morning mix of train track steel, a wet woods, and gray clouds. He took part, without remorse, in that first human response: think of yourself, Shine.

He thought he saw a wadded paper bag not far from the body.

It was a hand.

The purplish figure hardly exposed any fingers. Shine edged a few feet closer to the body. The person's face was unrecognizable. The only things that Shine could think of in those fleeting minutes where the sun's appearance only touched the tops of trees and nothing else were that this was a young person - probably a boy, given the short hair - and he had been crushed by a train at some point during the night.

And it happened so quickly, Shine thought, and in such darkness, that the train did not stop. If it had, cops and the firemen would have saturated this part of the train tracks down from Lefty's Tavern.

SHINE SWUNG AROUND HIS BIKE and jogged up the track toward Lefty's.

For a moment he stopped and stooped, leaning his head on the back tire, thinking he was about to gag. He soon hopped on his bike and embarked on a flighty list of plans that would not settle his mind. They were in no order. He wouldn't speak a word to anyone close to him for awhile about what he saw, especially to his girlfriend Cynthia and his sister Allison. He wouldn't tell his mother. He certainly wouldn't tell his father, who would return from Detroit soon, where his truck was filled with car transmission parts he was delivering to The Ford Motor Company auto plant.

Another plan, and this one was more sudden. He had twenty cents. He felt around in a pocket for a dime. He would speed out of Bedlam and toward Mt. Relling, and take a long way back to his house. At a phone booth near the public library in Relling, he would call the Bedlam police. It had to be reported.

He deliberated: Should I? Shouldn't I? What if I don't? What if I get caught? What do I say to a cop? What if someone saw me, and for whatever reason, I missed seeing somebody on a porch watching me, or missed somebody crossing the street who saw my bike?

Shine thought again of that one hand by itself. Its grotesqueness apart from the boy's body seemed encased in the incredible perfection of train tracks. That hand lay there encased inside the beauty of a long, cleared-out path of land so trains could move without obstruction.

His list of plans became clearer. They refreshed him with new energy as he picked up speed on his bike. He kept his head down as much as possible, his face barely noticeable. He zig-zagged along streets, feverishly avoiding any sign of a person who might later be able to identify his bike. The few people he saw walking toward the factories, offices, and stores seemed oblivious to his speed. He stayed as much as possible on side streets and weaved across cut-through alleys until he came to the phone booth.

In the booth's phone book, he looked up the number for Bedlam Police and dialed. On the other end, a sleepy voice answered. Shine never mentioned his name, and he'd decided he would not stay on the phone more than a minute.

"You saw a what?" the officer said.

"A body. It's down from Lefty's Tavern. Off to the side."

Shine cleared his throat. He stiffened his body to muster as deeply as possible a fake manly voice. His voice trembled. He thought he sounded more like an old lady.

"What's your name, sir?"

"Nevermind," Shine said.

"Look, if this is police business, I need a name. Your address, too."

"No."

"Don't say 'no' to me, sir. Please comply."

"No."

And then Shine faltered, completely flabbergasted by the officer's demands, and he became child-like apologetic. His jaws became tense, hard to move. He felt as if he was chewing glue. His mouth was dry.

"I don't mean to be mean, Mister Officer, I'm a good person." Shine stood so straight in that booth his thighs twitched. He kept a side of his face covered with one hand.

"How old are you?" the cop said.

"Just go look. Check out what I saw twenty minutes ago. Down by Lefty's. Hit by a train. I'm not lying."

"Your name, again? I'm asking one last time. And what were you doing on the train tracks?"

Shine slammed the phone on its holder. His hand trembled more than his voice. He felt like smoking. He felt the metal Band-Aid box in his back pocket which contained two or three last cigarettes. He wanted the convenience of an alley or a walkway in between buildings where he could light up and exhale some Kool cigarette smoke. Just to blow wreaths of smoke in the vacancy of an alley would help now. He would take quick puffs and hop back on his bike. He's then pop three peppermint Life-Savers into his mouth and head home.

But, in all his unluckiness, he saw other pedestrians and a few more bike-riders, now that the weekend morning emerged in full force.

He was trying hard to stop smoking, and he vowed to quit for his girlfriend Cynthia. He would. It might take a few more weeks. He wiped his sweaty forehead. He looked back at the phone booth and saw the phone must've bounced off the cradle. It dangled on its metal cord, still swaying above the phone book.

**

Made in the USA
Middletown, DE
02 August 2022

70269045R00054